The *Cam Jansen* Series

CAM JANSEN

and the
Mystery of the
Stolen Diamonds

★ ★

DAVID A. ADLER
Illustrated by Susanna Natti

★ ★

Viking

VIKING

A Division of Penguin Books USA Inc., 375 Hudson Street, New York, New York 10014
Penguin Books Ltd, 27 Wrights Lane, London W8 5TZ (Publishing & Editorial), and
Harmondsworth, Middlesex, England (Distribution & Warehouse)
Penguin Books Australia Ltd, Ringwood, Victoria, Australia
Penguin Books Canada Limited, 10 Alcorn Avenue, Toronto, Ontario, Canada M4V 3B2
Penguin Books (N.Z.) Ltd, 182–190 Wairau Road, Auckland 10, New Zealand

Text copyright © David A. Adler, 1980
Illustrations copyright © Susanna Natti, 1980
All rights reserved
First published in 1980 by Viking Penguin Inc.
Published simultaneously in Canada
Printed in the United States of America

3 5 7 9 10 8 6 4 2

Library of Congress Cataloging in Publication Data
Adler, David A.
Cam Jansen and the mystery of the stolen diamonds.
(Cam Jansen adventure series; v. 1)
Summary: A fifth-grader with a photographic memory, and her
friend Eric, help solve the mystery of the stolen diamonds.
[1. Mystery and detective stories] I. Natti, Susanna.
II. Title. III. Series.
PZ7.A2615Cam 1980   [Fic]   79-20695   ISBN 0-670-20039-5

To Deborah Brodie, a good friend

Cam Jansen and the
Mystery of the Stolen Diamonds

Chapter One

It was the first morning of spring vacation. Cam Jansen and her friend Eric Shelton were sitting on a bench in the middle of a busy shopping mall. While Eric's mother was shopping, they were watching Eric's baby brother, Howie. And they were playing a memory game.

Eric's eyes were closed.

"What color jacket am I wearing?" Cam asked.

"Blue."

"Wrong. I'm not wearing a jacket."

Eric opened his eyes. "It's no use," he said. "I'll never have a memory like yours."

"You have to keep practicing," Cam told him. "Now try me."

Cam looked straight ahead. She said, "*Click,*" and then closed her eyes. Cam always said, "*Click,*" when she wanted to remember something. She said it was the sound her mental camera made when it took a picture.

Eric looked for something he could be sure Cam hadn't noticed. Then he asked, "What does the sign in the card store window say?"

"That's easy. 'Mother's Day Sunday May 11. Remember your mother and she'll remember you.'"

"You win," Eric said.

Cam still had her eyes closed. "Come on, ask me something else."

Cam had what people called a photographic memory. Her mind took a picture

of whatever she saw. Once, she forgot her notebook in school. She did her home-work—ten math problems—all from the picture of the assignment she had stored in her brain.

When Cam was younger, people called her Jennifer. That's her real name. But when they found out about her amazing memory, they started calling her "The Camera." Soon "The Camera" was shortened to "Cam."

"All right," Eric said. "What color socks am I wearing?"

Cam thought a moment. "That's not really fair," she said. "I never saw your socks."

But Cam didn't open her eyes. "You're wearing green pants, a green belt, and green sneakers," she said. "I'll bet your socks are green, too."

"You're too much, Cam."

"No, you're too neat."

"It's my turn now," Eric said.

Eric looked carefully at all the stores and people in the shopping mall. He closed his eyes. But he quickly opened them again. Howie was crying.

"What do we do now?" Cam asked. "Should I look for your mother?"

6

Eric shook his head. "Let's wait. Maybe Howie will go back to sleep."

"But what if he doesn't?" Cam asked.

"Then I have to find out whether he wants to be held, fed, or changed. I have everything I need right here." Eric patted the insulated bag strapped to the front of the carriage.

Eric and Cam watched to see what Howie would do. He squirmed, turned his head from side to side, and then went back to sleep.

"Let's play another memory game," Cam said.

"Let's not. I'm tired of losing." Eric rocked the carriage. "Rocking relaxes a baby," he told Cam.

Cam was an only child so she didn't know much about babies. Eric was the oldest of four children. Besides Howie, who wasn't even a year old, Eric had twin sisters who were seven.

Eric rocked the carriage gently while he and Cam talked about the fifth-grade science fair. It was being held right after spring vacation. Eric was making a sundial, and Cam was making a box camera.

Suddenly a loud bell rang. It woke Howie and he started to cry.

Cam jumped up on the bench. "It's Parker's Jewelry Store!" she yelled. "Their alarm just went off."

Eric pulled at Cam's sneakers. "Get down from there."

"No, wait. Maybe something is happening."

Something *was* happening. A tall, heavy man with a mustache and wearing a dark suit ran out of the jewelry store toward the center of the mall. He was in a real hurry. He pushed people aside—including Eric. Cam looked straight at the man and said, *"Click."*

Chapter Two

The man kept running and caused a great commotion. He was bumping into dozens of people. He left a path of angry shoppers from Parker's Jewelry Store halfway through the shopping mall.

"Come back here, young man," one woman shouted, "and pick up all my packages!"

Another woman dropped a bag filled with groceries. Eggs broke. Tomatoes and cucumbers were rolling in all directions.

"If he's trying to get away," Cam asked,

"why didn't he run out one of the exits?"

"What?" Eric wasn't really listening. Howie was still crying, and Eric was trying to calm him.

Just then a young couple came out of the jewelry store.

"Look," Cam said. "They were inside when the alarm went off."

A small crowd had gathered. Cam was still standing on the bench. From there she had a good view of the entrance to Parker's.

The couple walked toward the nearest exit. The man was wearing a dark suit. He was tall, and so was the woman with him. She was holding what looked like a baby, wrapped in a pink blanket.

"There, there, baby," the woman was saying. "Don't cry. It's all over now. Don't cry."

The man was holding a very large pink-and-blue baby rattle. He was urging the

11

woman to walk faster. Cam looked straight
at them as they walked past, and said,
"Click."

Then Eric saw two old women coming
out of the store.

"Look," he said, pointing. "They were in
there, too, when the alarm went off."

12

The women were upset. One was clutching her heart. The other was leaning forward and holding a cane with both hands. She walked as if the cane were the only thing keeping her up.

The women sat down on the bench nearest Cam and Eric. "Oh, my," the woman holding her heart said. "I never thought I'd live through that."

The other woman just sighed.

Cam watched the entrance to Parker's a while longer. No one else left the store. Then she saw someone inside shut the door and hang a sign in the window. The sign said, "Sorry, We're Closed."

"I wonder what happened," Cam said as she got down from the bench.

Eric rocked Howie in his arms. "I don't know, but I wish they'd shut off that alarm. It's scaring Howie. I'll have to feed him if he doesn't stop crying."

Eric held Howie against his shoulder. Howie stopped crying, but just for a minute. A loud police car siren sounded. It startled Howie, and he began to cry again.

"Quick, Cam, get me his bottle. It's in the insulated bag."

Cam opened the bag and looked inside. "Boy, he sure needs a lot of stuff."

She gave the bottle to Eric. "Are you sure you know how to feed him?"

"It's easy. Watch."

14

Eric cradled Howie in one arm. With his free hand he fed him the bottle. Howie was quiet.

"It works," Cam said. "I guess he can't cry and drink at the same time."

The siren got louder and louder.

"They must have called the police," Cam said. She watched as the police car turned into the mall parking lot and slowed down. It stopped in front of Parker's Jewelry Store.

Both front doors of the car opened. Two policemen got out and went inside Parker's. A moment later the alarm over the store stopped ringing.

"They better hurry," Cam said, "or they won't catch the man who ran out."

The police did hurry. In a very short time they came out of Parker's. They went over to the people standing just outside the store.

"Please, we need your cooperation," one

of the policemen said. "Did any of you see a man run from here?"

Everyone started yelling at once.

"Yes, we saw him."

"He was tall."

"Heavy."

"No. No. He was short. Short and thin."

"He had a mustache."

"He was wearing an ugly green tie."

"Ugly! I liked that tie. I have the same one at home."

The policeman held up his hands for quiet. "Did any of you see which way he went?"

"I did," one woman called out. "He almost knocked me down." She put her hands on her hips and waited to make sure everyone was listening. "He went that way." She pointed toward the center of the mall.

One policeman ran to the center of the mall. The other reached into the car. He pulled out a police phone and spoke into it.

"Robbery reported at Parker's Jewelry Store, Hamilton Shopping Mall. Suspect, wearing dark suit and green tie, was last seen running toward Stage Street exit. Please send car to Stage and Fulton to help apprehend. Ten-four, central."

He reached into the car and replaced the phone. Then he ran toward the center of the mall.

Chapter Three

Cam sat down on the bench. She ran her fingers through her hair. Cam had what people called bright red hair even though it was more orange than red. Eric's hair was dark brown.

"Do you think they'll catch him?" Eric asked.

"It shouldn't be too hard," Cam said. "Almost everyone between here and the other end of the mall saw which way he went."

19

Eric was still feeding Howie. "Are you almost finished?" Cam asked.

"Almost."

"Good. Then we can go ask those two old women what happened inside the jewelry store."

Eric took the bottle out of Howie's mouth and set it down on the bench. He held Howie against his shoulder and patted his back. Howie burped.

"Okay," Eric announced. "We're ready."

Eric carried Howie, and Cam pushed the carriage. They went over to the next bench.

"My, what a cute baby," the woman with the cane said. "Is it a boy or a girl?"

"Boy."

The woman looked straight at Howie and asked, "Where's your mother, little boy?"

"He doesn't talk yet," Eric told her.

"Oh."

20

"I'm his brother. My mother took the twins shopping for clothes. I'm watching him until they're done."

"Clothes. Well, they're lucky they're not shopping for jewelry."

"Why?" Cam asked. "What happened inside the jewelry store?"

The woman put her hand to her cheek. She shook her head slowly. "Oh, it was horrible. We were there when a man came in and pointed a gun right at Mr. Parker. 'Diamonds,' he said. 'Every loose one you got.'

"Mr. Parker gave him a whole pile of small diamonds. You know, the kind he uses to make earrings. The man took them all. Then he made Mr. Parker lie face down on the floor.

"Isn't that right, Esther?"

"Yes," the other woman said, nodding her head. "He was terribly impolite."

"Then," the first woman went on, "he pointed his gun straight at us. He didn't dare talk to us the way he talked to Mr. Parker. He didn't rob us either. He just said, 'Ladies, turn around and face the wall and you won't get hurt.'

"There was a nice young couple in the store too. They had their baby with them, a cute little girl. I heard the man with the gun tell them to face the wall, too.

"It was horrible. We stayed that way,

22

with our faces to the wall, until Mr. Parker told us it was safe to leave."

The woman stopped talking. Someone was shouting. They all turned to see where the noise was coming from.

The policemen were coming back. There were four of them now. Handcuffed to one policeman was a tall man in a dark suit.

"I didn't do it!" the man yelled. "You've got the wrong man!"

"We'll let Mr. Parker decide that," the policeman said.

Cam was all excited. "That's him! They got him! That's the man who ran out of Parker's. I remember that mustache, that dark suit, and that ugly green tie."

"Well, he may be the man who ran out of the store," the woman with the cane declared, "but he's not the man who robbed Mr. Parker. Is he, Esther?"

"No. That's not him. I'm sure of it."

Chapter Four

Cam and Eric went back to their bench and sat down. Eric put Howie in the carriage and rocked him to sleep.

"Do you think those women are right?" Eric asked. "Do you think the police caught the wrong man?"

"The whole thing doesn't make sense," Cam said. "Whoever robbed the store pointed his gun straight at those women. They should know what he looks like. But if they're right and the man isn't the thief, why did he run like that?"

"Maybe you were wrong. Maybe he's not the man we saw running."

"Oh, he's the man all right," Cam said. "The man who ran past us had a mustache that curled up at the ends and an ugly green tie with red and yellow flowers. I'm sure that's the man the police caught."

The small crowd was gone. The only evidence that something had happened was the police car and the "Sorry, We're

Closed" sign in the window of the jewelry store. The four policemen and the man they caught were all inside Parker's.

Cam got up on the bench. She closed her eyes.

"What are you doing up there?" Eric asked.

"Thinking. This is where I was when everything happened. Standing here should help me remember what I saw."

"You know," Eric said, "there was another man who left the store, the man with the baby."

Cam sat down. "Yes, I know. I have a picture of him in my brain. He was tall and wore a dark suit just like the man the police caught. And he was holding a large baby rattle."

Cam thought for a minute. Then she went to the front of Howie's carriage and opened the insulated bag.

Cam spoke slowly, as if she were talking

and thinking at the same time. "There was something strange about that couple. Your mother packs this whole bag when she takes Howie somewhere. That couple had a baby too, but all they brought along was a rattle."

Cam stopped talking. Something was happening inside the store. Mr. Parker came to the window and turned the "closed" sign around. The other side of the sign said, "We're Open. Come in and Browse."

The door opened. The policemen came out with the man they had caught. He was no longer handcuffed. They spoke to him for just a moment. Then the man walked away. He walked past Cam and Eric and out the nearest exit. He smiled as he walked by.

"They let him go!" Cam said.

"Yeah, but did you see which way he went!"

Cam looked at Eric. They were both thinking the same thing.

"Before, when he was in such a rush, he went that way." Eric pointed to the center of the mall. "If he was in such a hurry to get there before, you'd think he'd go back that way now."

"Yeah," Cam said, "but he's going in the other direction. And it's the same way that couple went. Something strange is going on. Come on, let's follow him!"

"But what about Howie?"

"Bring him along."

Chapter Five

Cam and Eric quickly went out the Lee Avenue exit, the same one the man had gone through a few minutes earlier. It led to a street crowded with shoppers leaving the mall.

"Do you see him?" Eric asked.

"I think so. I think that's him up ahead. He's starting to walk down Lee Avenue."

Cam and Eric tried to get through the crowd quickly. With a baby carriage it wasn't easy.

They brushed past a woman carrying a

few large packages. She lost her balance,
and one of the packages fell.

"What do you think that is," she yelled,
pointing to the carriage, "a hot rod?"

Eric picked up the package. "I'm sorry,"
he told the woman.

"You should be, running through here
like that. I hope you don't have a baby in
there."

32

Eric was about to tell her there was a baby in the carriage. Cam didn't let him.

"Come on," she urged, "or we'll lose the man."

They rushed ahead. They turned the corner onto Lee Avenue and saw the man halfway down the block.

"Let's not get too close," Eric warned Cam, "or he'll know we're following him."

They were careful to keep a good distance behind the man. It didn't help. When the man reached the corner, he turned and looked straight at them.

"He saw us," Eric whispered. "What should we do?"

"Keep walking. If we stop whenever he does, he'll know we're following him."

The man stood still and waited. After Cam and Eric pushed the baby carriage past him, he turned and walked down Minnow Road.

Cam and Eric kept walking until the man

was out of sight. Then they turned and walked back to the corner of Minnow Road. The street was filled with construction equipment and huge mounds of dirt. A row of old houses was being torn down. Cam and Eric saw the man walk into the last house at the far end of the street.

"It's almost twelve," Eric said. "My mother will be waiting. Let's go back and call the police."

"And what would we tell them? If those women and Mr. Parker are right, we're following an innocent man. As soon as we know something we'll call."

Cam crouched and made her way down the street. "Come on," she called in a loud whisper.

Eric crouched, too, as he pushed Howie's carriage and followed Cam.

There were piles of dirt and sand all along the sidewalk. When they were behind a huge mound of dirt in front of the

34

last house, Cam collapsed. "We made it," she said.

"What do we do now?"

"Let's see what's going on inside that house."

Cam and Eric started to crawl up the dirt pile. Then Eric stopped. Howie was no longer sleeping. He was beginning to move in his carriage.

"Keep him quiet," Cam whispered.

"I'll try."

"You better do more than try. If he cries we're in real trouble."

Eric rocked the carriage gently. Howie looked up at Eric, but he didn't cry.

Cam reached the top of the dirt pile. She had a good view of the old house. It was three stories high with rows of windows. Some of the windows were broken. There were no curtains or shades. Cam could see right inside.

Through a large window on the first

floor she saw the man they had followed.
He wasn't alone. The couple who had left
the jewelry store just after the robbery was
there, too.

Cam quickly crawled down the hill. "I
was right, Eric."

"Sh." Eric pointed to Howie. "I think
he's going back to sleep."

"They're all in there," Cam whispered, "the Runner and the couple we saw leaving the store. They're all working together. The Runner made all that commotion to keep the police from catching the real thief."

"What about the woman and the baby?"

"Maybe they figured no one would suspect a man who went shopping with his wife and baby. If they did, they were right. You saw what happened when they left the store. They just walked away, and almost no one noticed."

"Let's go back now," Eric urged, "and get the police."

"You go," Cam told him, "and hurry! I'll stay here and watch the house."

"Watch Howie, too. I can move faster without him."

Eric ran off before Cam could tell him she didn't know how to watch a baby.

Cam sat back against the pile of dirt and

waited. It was very quiet. Cam looked around. Then she saw why it was so quiet. There were barriers at both ends of the street. Because houses were being torn down, cars were not allowed on Minnow Road.

Cam realized that she and Howie were alone. The only other people nearby were the thieves. *I hope Eric hurries,* Cam thought.

Whoosh!

Something dropped to the ground. Cam looked up. A squirrel running along the branch of a tree had dropped an acorn.

Howie started to cry. *Oh, no!* Cam thought. *What would Eric do?*

Cam said, *"Click."* Sometimes just saying it helped her remember. It did. Cam remembered the insulated bag and that Howie couldn't drink milk and cry at the same time. She took the bottle out of the bag.

Then Cam heard another noise. She dropped the bottle and looked up. This time it wasn't a squirrel.

Chapter Six

A big tall man was standing on top of the mound of dirt. He was wearing an ugly green tie and had a mustache that curled up at the ends. It was the Runner.

"Well," he growled, "look who we have here—the baby sitter and her baby. Where's your friend?"

"He . . . he went home."

"If you were smart you would've done the same thing. Let's go."

Cam carried Howie up the front steps of the house. Inside, the house was musty.

The floor was covered with dust and littered with old newspapers and magazines. The Runner took Cam and Howie into a large room.

"Look what I got," the Runner said. "It's one of the kids I saw following me."

A man and a woman looked up. It was the couple Cam had seen leaving Parker's Jewelry Store. They were sitting in worn, old-fashioned easy chairs. There was a small table between them.

"You said there were two of them," the sitting man snapped. "Where's the other one?"

"He wasn't out there," the Runner said.

"Great! Everything was perfect until you get yourself followed. Well, watch this kid. Don't let her get away."

The Runner nudged Cam and Howie into a corner. He stood there watching them. Cam looked at the thieves and was frightened.

"Let's divide this stuff and get out of here," the sitting man said.

He took a large baby rattle out of his pocket. It was the rattle he was carrying as he left the store. He screwed off the top and carefully emptied the contents onto the table.

"Wow!" the woman said.

That was exactly how Cam felt. The rattle was filled with diamonds. They sparkled as the man started to count them.

"One, two, three . . ."

Cam held Howie close and looked around the room. In the back, pulled away from the wall, were a few large bookcases. There were windows behind the bookcases. And there was an open door, which led to another room.

Cam looked at the thieves. Something was missing. She whispered, *"Click,"* and tried to remember what it was.

The baby, she thought. *Where's the baby?*

Then Cam noticed something on the floor wrapped in a pink blanket. It was a large doll. Cam realized that there never was a baby. That's why the couple hadn't been carrying any of the things Eric's mother packed in the insulated bag. The thieves had taken the doll along so they would look like a family. And the rattle was a good place to hide the diamonds.

The man was still counting. "Fifty-eight, fifty-nine, sixty . . ."

45

Cam looked at her watch. It was 12:30. *Where's Eric?* she thought. *Maybe he can't get the police to come.*

"Seventy-nine, eighty, eighty-one. We got eighty-one diamonds," the man announced.

"Let's see now," he said as he did some figuring on an old newspaper. "That's eighty-one divided by three. Hmm. That gives each of us twenty-one. No, that's not right." He did some more figuring.

"Twenty-seven," the woman said. "We each get twenty-seven."

The Runner left Cam's side and went to get his diamonds.

I can't wait for Eric, Cam thought. *This is my chance.*

She held Howie tight and ran to the door in the back of the room. She slammed the door shut as if she were leaving the room. Then she jumped behind the nearest bookcase.

46

"Get her!" someone yelled.

Cam hoped her trick would work. She couldn't see what was happening, but she heard doors opening and closing and a lot of yelling.

"Find her!"

"I'm looking."

"Check the back room."

The trick did work. The thieves thought she had left the room. They were looking all over the house for her.

Cam knew she couldn't stay behind that bookcase forever. Eventually the thieves would find her. She looked at Howie. His eyes were open. *Or you might cry,* Cam thought.

There was a window behind the bookcase. Cam tried to open it. She couldn't. It was jammed.

The window behind the next bookcase was open, but to get to it Cam would have to run past a large open area. Cam didn't know if anyone else was in the room. She was afraid to run out in the open.

Someone ran past the bookcase.

"What about the kitchen?"

"I've already looked there."

"Look again."

Howie began to stir. *Oh, no!* Cam thought. *He's getting ready to cry!*

Chapter Seven

The *bottle!* Cam thought. *I should have taken it along. That would keep him quiet.*

Then Cam had an idea. She gently pushed the tip of her finger into Howie's mouth. The baby was quiet as he sucked on Cam's finger.

Cam heard footsteps. One of the men was standing very close.

"You check the cellar," the man yelled. "I'll look in here."

Cam heard the man move slowly around

the room. Then it was quiet. Cam wondered where the man had gone.

"Psst . . . Psst."

The sound came from behind. Cam was afraid to look.

"Psst . . . Psst. Over here. Hurry."

It didn't sound like one of the thieves. Cam turned. Through the open window behind the next bookcase she saw the head and shoulders of a policeman. He was sig-

naling for Cam to run over and climb out.

Cam held Howie tightly. She ran past the open area, then squeezed into the small space between the window and the bookcase. She handed Howie to the policeman. Then she climbed out and jumped to the ground.

Eric ran up and took Howie in his arms. Howie looked at the policeman, then at Eric, then back at the policeman. Then Howie started to cry.

Cam smiled. "Boy, am I glad he didn't do that inside!"

"Yes, I'm sure you are," the policeman said.

Another policeman ran up to them. He was carrying a megaphone.

"How many of them are in there?"

"Three. Two men and a woman."

"That's what your friend told us."

Cam and Eric went behind one of the police cars. "I'm sure glad you're all right,"

Eric said. "I got back here as fast as I could."

The policeman held the megaphone to his mouth. "This is the police. The house is surrounded. Come out with your hands up."

Cam looked around. The house *was* surrounded. She saw about fifteen policemen and four other police cars parked around the house.

"Come out with your hands up and you won't get hurt."

The back door opened. First the woman came out and then the two men. They all had their hands up. The policemen handcuffed them and led them into one of the police cars.

Chapter Eight

One of the policemen drove Cam, Eric, and Howie back to the shopping mall. Howie's carriage was tied to the roof of the car.

"You must be 'The Camera,'" the policeman said to Cam. "Your friend told us about your amazing memory.

"Well, it's lucky you were in the mall," the policeman went on. "Those thieves had us baffled. Mr. Parker told us there was only one thief. So, of course, we chased the one man who ran. Mr. Parker was lying on the floor. Those two old ladies were facing the wall. None of them saw the thief join up with a woman and pretend to be part of a young family out shopping."

The policeman drove the car through the shopping mall parking lot. He parked it right in front of Parker's Jewelry Store. Eric's mother and sisters were waiting for them. So were the two old women.

As soon as the police car stopped, Eric's mother ran over and opened the door. She quickly took Howie in her arms.

"Eric and Jennifer, it's one o'clock. Where have you been?"

"Your mother has been worried sick," the old woman with the cane said.

"These two are heroes," the policeman said, pointing to Cam and Eric. "They helped us capture the gang that robbed the jewelry store."

"You know," the woman with the cane said, "there was a nice young couple in Par-

ker's when the store was robbed. I re-member that cute baby they had. Well, someone should tell them the robbers have been caught. They may be worried."

"Nice couple!" Cam yelled. Then she laughed. Eric and the policeman laughed, too.

CAM JANSEN
and the
Mystery of the
Babe Ruth Baseball

★ ★

DAVID A. ADLER
Illustrated by Susanna Natti

★ ★

Viking

VIKING

Published by the Penguin Group

Penguin Books USA Inc., 375 Hudson Street, New York, New York 10014, U.S.A.

Penguin Books Ltd, 27 Wrights Lane, London W8 5TZ, England

Penguin Books Australia Ltd, Ringwood, Victoria, Australia

Penguin Books Canada Ltd, 10 Alcorn Avenue, Toronto, Ontario, Canada M4V 3B2

Penguin Books (N.Z.) Ltd, 182–190 Wairau Road, Auckland 10, New Zealand

Penguin Books Ltd, Registered Offices: Harmondsworth, Middlesex, England

Library of Congress Cataloging in Publication Data

Adler, David A.   Cam Jansen and the mystery of the Babe Ruth baseball.

(Cam Jansen adventure)

Summary: Cam uses her photographic memory to identify the person
who stole a valuable autographed baseball.

[1. Mystery and detective stories.   2. Baseball—Fiction]

I. Natti, Susanna, ill. II. Title. III. Series: Adler, David A.

Cam Jansen adventure.

PZ7.A2615Cab   [Fic]   82-2621   ISBN 0-670-20037-9   AACR2

To Bette and Simeon Guterman
with love

Cam Jansen and the
Mystery of the Babe Ruth Baseball

Chapter One

It was a Sunday afternoon at the end of May. Cam Jansen and her friend Eric Shelton were in the local community center. A hobby show was being held there, and Cam's parents had brought their collection of circus posters.

Cam's father fixed his bow tie. He looked at his watch and said, "It's almost time."

"You should go now, before you miss it," Cam's mother added.

Cam and Eric rushed to the clock corner, where there were more than twenty cuckoo clocks hanging on the wall. It was almost four o'clock. Cam and Eric waited. Then the noise started. When the minute hand of each clock reached twelve, a tiny door opened and a small wooden bird popped out. "Cuckoo, cuckoo, cuckoo, cuckoo," it chirped.

All the birds seemed to be coming out of all the clocks at once. People in the large room turned to look at the clocks. Many of them looked at their watches to see if it really was four o'clock.

After the clock doors had closed, Cam and Eric looked at some of the other exhibits. They looked at needlepoint pillows, the Collins Coin Shop exhibit, a display of old toys, and at a large collection of baseball cards, yearbooks, and posters.

"Look here," Eric said. "There's a whole section about Babe Ruth."

There were a few Babe Ruth baseball cards, some photographs, a baseball the

4

Babe had autographed, and a large poster of Babe Ruth hitting a home run. The poster also listed his record as a player.

"Test my memory," Cam told Eric. "Ask me anything about Babe Ruth's playing record."

Cam looked carefully at all the numbers on the poster. Then she closed her eyes and said, *"Click."* Cam always says, *"Click,"* when she wants to remember something. When people ask her why, she points to her head and tells them, "This is a mental camera. Just like any camera, it goes *'click'* when it takes a picture."

"What was the Babe's real name?" Eric asked.

"George Herman Ruth," Cam said with her eyes still closed.

"How many games did he play in 1924?"

"One hundred and fifty-three."

Cam has what people call a photographic memory. Her mind takes a picture of whatever she sees. When she wants to remember something, even a detail such as how many games Babe Ruth played in any one year, she just looks at the photograph stored in her brain.

Cam's real name is Jennifer Jansen. But when people found out about her amazing memory, they called her "The Camera." Soon "The Camera" was shortened to "Cam."

"When did Babe Ruth get the most hits?" Eric asked.

"In 1923. He had two hundred and five hits that year. And he hit the most home runs in 1927. That's when he hit sixty," Cam said, with her eyes still closed.

The owner of the collection was listening. He was an old man. He had a bushy white mustache, and he was wearing a baseball cap.

"You really know all about baseball," the old man said.

Cam opened her eyes and said, "No, I don't. I just remember everything on that poster."

Then Eric told him, "She has a mental camera. Why don't you test her?"

The old man picked up a box of baseball cards. "Take a card," he called to the people around the exhibit. "We'll see how good this girl's memory *really* is."

Two people reached into the box and took out a card. Cam looked at the people. Then she looked at the cards they were holding. She said, *"Click,"* and closed her eyes.

"What card am I holding?" a teenage boy wearing jeans and a bright green jacket asked.

"You're holding a Reggie Jackson card."

"That's right," the boy said. Then he looked at his card and asked, "How many doubles did he hit in 1977?"

"Thirty-nine."

A girl with long brown hair, holding a large gym bag, asked, "What card am I holding? When was the player born and what's his middle name?"

"It's a Stan Musial card. He was born in 1920, on November twenty-first, and his full name is Stanley Frank Musial."

"Amazing!" the man said as Cam opened her eyes. He told her that his name was Henry Baker, and he asked Cam and Eric if they could come back later. He wanted his wife to meet Cam and test her memory.

"Sure, I can come back," Cam told him.

"Oh, good. Now let me show you my collection."

Mr. Baker showed Cam and Eric his favorite baseball cards. He showed them cards of Billy Martin, Fernando Valenzuela, Ron Guidry, and Satchel Paige. After that, he led Cam and Eric to the Babe Ruth corner.

He showed them his Babe Ruth cards. Then Mr. Baker said, "Wait till you see

10

this. I have a baseball that Babe Ruth signed for me almost fifty years ago."

Mr. Baker turned around. The wooden stand the baseball had rested on was there, but the baseball was gone.

Chapter Two

"Someone stole my baseball!" Mr. Baker cried out.

A woman nearby looked at him. She laughed and said, "Ask your mommy to get you another one."

"This wasn't just any baseball. Babe Ruth signed it. He gave it to me when I was a boy. It's very valuable."

Mr. Baker ran from one person to the next, asking, "Have you seen my baseball? Did you see it rolling on the floor? Did you see someone take it?"

Eric looked on the floor for the ball. Cam stood on a chair to watch what Mr. Baker was doing.

"He's so upset," Cam told Eric. "He's stopping everyone. Most of them think he's crazy."

While Cam stood on the chair, she looked across the exhibit hall. She saw her parents with a large circus poster hanging behind them. She saw the wall of cuckoo clocks. Then she saw someone leaving the exhibit hall. It was a teenage boy wearing a bright green jacket. Cam closed her eyes and said, *"Click."*

"Let's go!" Cam shouted to Eric when she opened her eyes. "Someone's leaving the hall, and he might have the baseball."

Cam ran between two women trading rare postage stamps. She crawled under a few tables and almost knocked over a small boy looking at some old toys.

Eric followed Cam. "I'm sorry. Excuse me," he said to the two women and the small boy as he hurried past.

When Cam got to the door she told the guard, "You have to stop him!"

"What are you talking about?"

"That boy in the green jacket. He was

there when a valuable baseball was stolen. The baseball was in the exhibit, and I'm sure that boy took it. That's why he's in such a rush to get out of here."

"Just because he's leaving the hall doesn't mean he's a thief," the guard said.

The boy in the green jacket turned and saw Cam talking to the guard. He started to run.

"Did you see that!" Eric said. "He saw us talking to you and he started to run."

The boy ran around the corner of the building. He was out of sight.

"We'll never catch him now," Cam said.

"Yes, we will," the guard said.

He ran after the boy. Cam and Eric followed him.

They ran to a crowded playground on the other side of the building. Two young children were playing catch with a baseball. Others were jumping rope or playing basketball. In one corner of the playground some parents were watching very young children playing in a large sandbox, on seesaws, or on swings.

The guard ran with Cam and Eric until they got to the other end of the playground.

"He's gone," Cam said. "I don't see him anywhere."

They looked down the street leading

16

from the playground. A few children were walking there. A man was pushing a baby carriage, and there were some people waiting at the bus stop. But no one was wearing a bright green jacket.

"There's another way out of the playground," the guard said. He turned and started to walk toward the other exit. Then he stopped.

"Is that him?" the guard asked, pointing to a boy sitting on one of the park benches.

Chapter Three

The boy sitting on the bench was wearing jeans and a bright green jacket. He was sitting behind the two children who were playing catch.

"Yes, that's him," Cam said.

Cam, Eric, and the guard ran to the bench. The boy looked up at them. He smiled and said, "Well, look who's here. It's the girl with the amazing memory and her quiet friend."

"A valuable baseball is missing from one

18

of the exhibits," the guard told the boy. "We're looking for it."

"I'm sorry, but I don't know where it is."

Cam looked at the boy. There was something in one of his jacket pockets. It was round and about the size of a baseball.

Cam closed her eyes and said, *"Click."* She looked at the picture in her mind of the boy when he was holding the Reggie Jackson baseball card.

Cam opened her eyes and said, "What's that in your pocket? It wasn't there before."

"Oh, this," the boy said, and reached into his pocket. "You just didn't notice it."

He took out a baseball and showed it to the guard.

"This can't be the missing baseball," the guard said. "It's not signed by Babe Ruth. It says 'Little League Slugger.'"

The guard turned to Cam and Eric and said, "I don't know why I listened to you. Maybe there never was any Babe Ruth baseball. Now I have to get back to the exhibit hall. But first I think you owe this boy an apology."

Cam and Eric told the boy that they were sorry. The guard walked back to the exhibit hall. Cam and Eric walked to a bench on the other side of the playground and sat down.

Cam and Eric lived next door to each

other. They were in the same fifth grade class, and they spent a lot of time together. Eric knew that Cam wouldn't give up the search for the missing baseball so quickly. She didn't.

"Where did he get that ball? He didn't have it when we saw him at Mr. Baker's exhibit."

"Maybe he found it," Eric said.

"Maybe."

Cam closed her eyes. She said, "*Click.*" Then she added, "I'm trying to remember everything I saw at the exhibit."

While Cam's eyes were closed, Eric looked around the playground. He saw a side door to the exhibit hall open.

"Cam, look! Isn't that the girl we saw at Mr. Baker's exhibit?"

Cam opened her eyes. She looked at the girl leaving the exhibit hall. The girl had long brown hair and was carrying a gym bag.

"Yes. That's her. And there's enough
room in that gym bag for twenty baseballs.
I'll bet she left through the side door so no
one would see her."

The girl walked past Cam and Eric, but
she didn't notice them. She walked out of
the playground. At the corner she crossed
the street and walked toward the bus stop.

"Come on," Cam said. "Let's follow her."

Cam and Eric had to wait at the corner for the traffic light to turn green. As they waited, the girl got farther and farther ahead. When the light changed, Cam and Eric ran to get closer. The girl turned and saw them. She began running, too.

The girl held the gym bag with both hands as she ran. She ran past the bus stop. She turned and saw Cam and Eric behind her. She looked scared.

At the corner the girl quickly looked to see if any cars were coming. Then she ran across the street.

"Let's rest," Eric said to Cam when they reached the corner.

"No. We have to catch her. I'm sure she took the baseball. That's why she's running."

Cam and Eric crossed the street and chased the girl. She was halfway down the block when her gym bag dropped from her

hands. The girl tripped over the bag and fell.

Cam and Eric caught up with the girl. She was still lying on the sidewalk. The girl held her gym bag up and said, "Here, take what you want. Just don't hurt me."

Chapter Four

"We're not going to hurt you," Eric told the girl.

Cam took the bag from the girl's hands and said, "We're just going to take the Babe Ruth baseball you stole and give it back to Mr. Baker."

"I didn't steal any baseball."

"Then why were you running?"

"I was running because you were chasing me."

"We'll see," Cam said as she opened the bag.

26

"Wait," Eric said. "It's her bag. We can't look through it unless she says we can."

The girl sat up and said, "Look all you want. You'll see that I didn't steal anything."

Cam reached into the bag. She took out an old newspaper, a puzzle book about outer space, and a dried-up slice of cheese.

"You should really wrap cheese in plastic or foil," Eric told the girl.

Cam reached into the bag again and took out an apple, an empty soda can, and a roller skate. She felt along the bottom of the bag.

"There's no baseball in here, but there sure are a lot of papers."

"Maybe my book report is in there. I wrote it last week, but I can't remember where I put it."

Eric helped the girl up. Cam gave the gym bag back to her and said, "I'm sorry we chased you. And I'm sorry we thought you stole that baseball."

"That's all right," the girl said as she looked through the papers in her bag. "It will be worth it if I find that book report."

The girl took old comic books, crushed homework papers, and candy wrappers from the bag. Cam and Eric left her and started walking toward the exhibit hall. When they reached the corner, the girl waved some papers at them and called out, "I found it! I found it!"

"I'm glad we helped find *something*," Cam said to Eric. "But I wish it had been the baseball."

When Cam and Eric reached the playground, they sat down on one of the benches. Eric watched the children playing basketball.

Cam closed her eyes and said, *"Click."* She thought for a moment. She said, *"Click,"* a few more times. Then she opened her eyes.

"The baseball was there when we first came to the exhibit, but it was gone a few minutes later. So it must have been taken while we were there," Cam said. "I just wish I had a picture of who was standing in the Babe Ruth corner when the ball was taken."

Eric wasn't looking at Cam while she talked to him. He was looking across the playground.

"The one thing that I don't understand," Eric said, "is why that boy ran from the hall. He was in a real hurry then, but he didn't go anywhere. He's still sitting there on that bench."

Cam looked across the playground. Then she closed her eyes and said, *"Click."*

Cam told Eric, "I'm looking at the picture

30

I have of him at the exhibit. He said he had a baseball in his pocket the whole time, but that's not true. He didn't have it in his pocket when we first saw him."

Cam opened her eyes and asked, "What is he doing over there?"

"It looks like he's watching those two children playing catch."

Cam looked across the playground at the boy in the green jacket. She thought for a minute. Then she clapped her hands together and said, "That's it! I think I know where the Babe Ruth baseball is."

"Where?"

Cam started to explain, but then she saw something that made her stop.

"Look at that," she said, and pointed across the playground. "Now I *know* where the baseball is."

Chapter Five

Cam was pointing to the two children
playing catch. One of them had thrown the
ball too far. The boy in the green jacket was
picking it up.

"Did you see that?" Cam asked.

"See what?"

"He picked up their baseball. Now I bet
he'll switch baseballs. He'll throw back the
one he has in his pocket."

The boy in the green jacket turned
around. As he turned, he took the baseball
out of his pocket and threw it over his head

to the two children. Then he started to walk away.

"Come on, Eric. Let's follow him."

"Why? What's the difference if he did switch baseballs? Those children couldn't have the Babe Ruth ball. They were outside when it was stolen."

The boy in the green jacket walked quickly away from the playground. He didn't even look as he crossed the street.

Horns honked. Two cars stopped short to avoid hitting him. But the boy didn't even turn around.

Cam ran through the playground and out the exit. Eric followed her. They waited at the corner and then crossed the street when they were sure no cars were coming. The boy was almost a full block ahead of them.

"Let's be careful," Cam told Eric. "I don't want that boy to know we're following him."

Cam and Eric stayed about half a block behind the boy. They walked past a row of stores. At the corner the boy turned around. He looked straight at Cam and Eric.

"Quick!" Cam said. "Let's go into one of these stores."

It was Sunday. The only place open was a small food store. Cam opened the door, and Eric quickly followed her inside.

34

"Can I help you?" a man behind the counter asked.

"No. We don't need anything," Cam told him.

"Of course you do. Now try to remember what your mother sent you to get. Was it milk? We have regular milk, ninety-nine-

percent-fat-free milk, skim milk, and but-termilk."

"We don't need milk," Eric said.

"Maybe you came for bread or canned vegetables. We have peas, spinach, corn, car-rots, and lima beans."

Cam opened the door and looked out-side. Then she told Eric, "Let's go before we lose him."

"Maybe you need juice," the man called as Cam and Eric were leaving. "We have orange juice, apple juice, tomato juice, grapefruit juice, and lemon juice."

When Cam and Eric stepped outside the store, they looked for the boy. He was gone. They ran to the corner. They looked ahead and down both side streets.

"There he is," Eric said.

The boy was walking down one of the side streets. Cam and Eric were careful not to get too close. There were a few stores along the first half of the block. The rest of the block was lined with apartment buildings. They saw the boy walk into one of the buildings.

Cam and Eric ran to the building. They peeked into the lobby. The boy was standing there waiting for the elevator. He got into the elevator, and the doors closed behind him.

Cam and Eric ran into the building. They watched the numbers over the elevator door light up. Number five stayed lit for a long time.

"He got off on the fifth floor," Cam told Eric. "Now we know where he lives. I'll stay here and watch to make sure he doesn't leave. You go get the police."

"No!"

"No?"

"You still haven't told me why we followed him. What will I tell the police?"

Cam sat on one of the chairs in the lobby. Eric sat next to her.

"While we were sitting in the playground, I looked at the pictures I have
stored in my head. That boy didn't have a
ball in his pocket when we first saw him at
the exhibit. But he did have one when we
saw him later."

"But it wasn't the Babe Ruth baseball."

38

"I know it wasn't. At first that confused me. Then I saw a ball get away from those two children playing catch. When the boy picked it up, I knew what had happened."

"What?"

"That boy took the Babe Ruth ball from the exhibit. He saw us speaking to the guard so he ran. But then he had a better idea. The ball the two children were playing with must have landed near him. That was the first time he switched the baseballs. The two children didn't know it, but they were playing catch with a very valuable baseball."

Eric stood up and said, "Then, while we were watching, he switched the baseballs again. Now he has the Babe Ruth ball."

Eric walked toward the door. As he was leaving the building, he said to Cam, "You wait right here. I'll go and get the police."

"And tell my parents where I am," Cam said.

Cam waited until she was sure that Eric was gone. Then she walked over and pushed the button for the elevator. When it came, she got on and pressed the button for the fifth floor.

Chapter Six

The elevator stopped on the third floor. A woman was standing there reading a flier about the items on sale at the local supermarket. She got into the elevator and asked, "Are you going down?"

"No. I'm going up," Cam answered.

The woman smiled and said, "That's all right. I'll come along for the ride."

The doors closed and the elevator started to move.

The elevator stopped on the fifth floor and Cam got off. The hall was lined with doors. *What will I tell the police?* Cam wondered. *How will they know which is the boy's apartment?*

Cam looked at the names on each of the doors: Benson, Jackson, Goldwin, Cruz, Washington, Hamada, Grant, and Keller.

Maybe his name is Benson, Cam thought. *He looked like a Benson. Or maybe he's a Keller.*

A door opened. It was the door to the Goldwin apartment. As the door opened, a

paper fell to the floor. It was a flier just like the one the woman in the elevator had had. Cam looked at a few of the other apartment doors. Each one had a folded flier pressed into the frame of the door.

A tall woman with red hair just like Cam's came out of the Goldwin apartment. Two children were with her. One of the children, a small boy with curly blond hair, picked up the flier. As they walked to the elevator, the woman smiled at Cam.

Cam waited until they were in the elevator. Then she walked from one apartment door to the next. Two of them, the Goldwins' and the Grants', did not have fliers.

His name is Grant, Cam said to herself. *He must have taken the flier when he went inside.*

Cam was just about to knock on the door when she heard some people get off the elevator. It was Cam's parents and Eric, with a policeman and a policewoman.

"Why didn't you wait for us downstairs?" Eric asked.

"His name is Grant," Cam told them. "This is his apartment."

"What were you about to do?" Cam's father asked.

"I hope you weren't going to knock on the door," Cam's mother said. "Chasing and catching a thief isn't something children should do. It's a job for the police."

The policeman knocked on the door.

"Who is it?" a voice called from inside the apartment.

"It's the police. We'd like to ask a few questions."

The door was opened by a boy wearing jeans.

"Is this the boy you think took the baseball?" the policeman asked.

"Yes," Cam told him.

"No!" the boy shouted. "You're wasting your time. This is the second time these

44

two kids have said I stole that baseball. I had one with me when I left the exhibit, but it wasn't the Babe Ruth ball. I showed it to them the last time."

"Would you please show it to us?" the policewoman asked.

"Just a minute."

The boy opened a closet near the front door of the apartment. Then he held out a baseball.

Cam looked at the ball. She closed her eyes and said, *"Click."*

"This isn't the same one you showed us in the park," Cam said when she opened her eyes.

"Is this the Babe Ruth baseball?" the policewoman asked.

"No."

"Then let's go."

The boy was just closing the apartment door when something green caught Cam's eye. The boy's jacket was hanging over the back of a kitchen chair. And there was something on the kitchen table.

"Wait," Cam said. "Don't close the door."

Chapter Seven

Cam's father held the door open.

"What is it now?" the policewoman asked Cam.

"I saw the baseball. It's on the kitchen table."

"Are you sure?"

"I think I'm sure."

The policewoman looked inside the apartment. "Oh, there *is* a baseball on the table," she said. "Bring it here," she told the boy.

The boy walked slowly to the kitchen. He

took the baseball off the table and brought it to the policewoman.

"It sure is old," the policewoman said as she looked at the ball. "And it says here 'To Henry Baker, from The Babe.'"

"Maybe it's mine," the boy said.

"Is it?" the policewoman asked.

"Well, no," the boy said softly. "I took it from the old man. I'm sorry."

"You'll have to come to the police station with us. We'll call your parents," the policewoman said as she led the boy to the elevator.

"But first we'll stop at the exhibit," the policeman said. "We'll return the baseball to Mr. Baker."

They all squeezed into the police car. The boy just stared quietly out of the car window. But the police officers and Cam's parents weren't quiet at all. They talked all during the ride to the exhibit hall.

"I'm too young to remember the great

Babe Ruth," the policewoman said. "But my father told me lots of stories about him.

"His favorite story was about the time Babe Ruth hit a home run in the 1932 World Series. The score was tied. There were two strikes. The Babe pointed to the centerfield fence. Then . . ." She paused.

"And then what happened?" asked Cam's mother.

"That's where he hit the very next pitch, right over the centerfield fence."

"And on the *next* pitch," the policeman said, "Lou Gehrig hit a home run."

"He was a pretty good ballplayer, too," Cam's father said.

When they reached the exhibit hall, Cam, her parents, Eric, and the police-woman went inside. Cam held the baseball with both hands.

Mr. Baker was sitting in the Babe Ruth corner of the exhibit. His head was down.

Eric tapped him on the shoulder. Then
Cam gave him the baseball.

"You found it! You found it!" Mr. Baker
yelled. He hugged Cam, Cam's father, Eric,
the policewoman, and a man who just happened to be walking past.

"Look, they found my baseball!" Mr.

Baker told his wife when she came from the other side of the exhibit.

"I'm not putting this back on display," Mr. Baker said as he put the baseball in his pocket. "Someone else might take it."

"I want you to come to the station house and sign a complaint against the boy who took it," the policewoman said. "Come as soon as the exhibit closes."

The policewoman started to leave.

"Wait," Mr. Baker said. He took a handful of baseball cards from the box. "Take this," he said as he handed the policewoman a card. "It's Hank Aaron. He's the greatest home run hitter of all time. And here's George Brett and Yogi Berra and Willie Mays and Pete Rose."

The policewoman held up her hands and said, "Oh, thank you, but don't give them to me. Give them to these two children. They're the ones who found your baseball."

Mr. Baker gave the cards to Cam and Eric.

"Can you stay a little longer?" he asked Cam. "My wife would like to see you and your amazing mental camera at work."

"Sure."

"Good. Wait right here. I want everyone to see what a great memory you have."

Chapter Eight

"**M**ay I have your attention, please," a woman's voice called out over the loudspeaker. "First, I want to thank you for coming to our hobby show. And I want to invite all of you to go to Henry Baker's baseball exhibit. An amazing memory show will be given there in just a few minutes."

A small crowd gathered around Mr. Baker's exhibit. Cam's parents stood right near the front. Both of them were tall and thin. Cam's father had red hair just like

Cam. Cam's mother's hair was brown and curly.

Mr. Baker and Cam were standing on chairs. Mr. Baker quietly asked Cam a few questions. Then he announced, "The girl standing next to me is Jennifer Jansen. She is in the fifth grade, and she has a remarkable memory."

Mr. Baker picked up a box and said, "I'm going to pick a few cards from this box. Jennifer will take a quick look at the cards. Then I'll let you test her memory."

Mr. Baker picked out some cards and handed them to Cam. Cam said, *"Click,"* as she looked at each card. Then she gave the cards to Eric and closed her eyes.

Eric gave the cards to people in the crowd. "Ask her anything you want," Eric told them.

"I'm holding a Dave Winfield card," someone called out. "What's his middle name?"

"Mark."

"What's Eddie Murray's hobby?"

"Basketball."

A woman standing next to Cam's parents said, "She sure has an amazing memory."

Cam's mother told the woman, "She's our daughter. We're very proud of her."

"And not just because of her memory," Cam's father said. "We were proud of her even before she said her first *'Click.'* "